This adventure belongs to

- - - - - - - - - - - - - - - - - - -

TO ALL THOSE WHO HAVE EVER FELT A BIT DIFFERENT.

WITH ENDLESS THANKS
TO MY FAMILY

First published 2012 by Walker Books Ltd
87 Vauxhall Walk, London SE11 5HJ

10 9 8 7 6 5 4 3 2 1

Birgitta Sif © 2012

The right of Birgitta Sif to be identified as author/illustrator
of this work has been asserted by her in accordance
with the Copyright, Designs and Patents Act 1988

This book has been typeset in Joe Regular

Printed in China

British Library Cataloguing in Publication Data: a catalogue record
for this book is available from the British Library

ISBN 978-1-4063-3797-6

www.walker.co.uk

WALKER BOOKS
AND SUBSIDIARIES
LONDON • BOSTON • SYDNEY • AUCKLAND

Oliver

Birgitta Sif

Oliver felt a bit different.

But it didn't matter.
He lived in his own world,
happily, with his friends.

They had lots of adventures together.

They searched for treasure and rode camels through the desert.

They crossed narrow bridges and bravely fought sharks.

They jumped over oceans and slid down waterfalls.

They even visited the other side of the world.

But sometimes there were
things Oliver had to do
on his own.

And sometimes, wherever he was,
he wanted to fly away.

One evening, he played
the piano for his friends,

but no one listened.

Oliver felt a bit different.

The next day, as he was playing
a tennis match on his own ...

the ball flew over his head ...

and bounced ... and bounced ... and rolled ... and rolled away.

So Oliver set off on
another adventure,

through the wild jungle,
over the river,

up and up
the mountain,

until he found a narrow gate
to somewhere new.

It was the beginning of the
best adventure he'd ever had.

Oliver was a bit different.

But it didn't matter.

Olivia was
a bit different too.